Daddy's
ROCK HOUND

written by:

Malinda Rowe Kallimani

tate publishing
CHILDREN'S DIVISION

Published by Tate Publishing & Enterprises, LLC
127 E. Trade Center Terrace | Mustang, Oklahoma 73064 USA
1.888.361.9473 | www.tatepublishing.com

Tate Publishing is committed to excellence in the publishing industry. The company reflects the philosophy established by the founders, based on Psalm 68:11,
"The Lord gave the word and great was the company of those who published it."

Book design copyright © 2016 by Tate Publishing, LLC. All rights reserved.
Cover and interior design by Rhezette Fiel
Illustrations by Joshua Aquino

Published in the United States of America

ISBN: 978-1-68293-525-5
1. Juvenile Fiction / Nature & The Natural World / General
2. Juvenile Fiction / Family / Parents
16.01.20

To my father,

Kenneth Howard Rowe,

who always found enjoyment in the
simple things in life

My daddy always liked rocks. When we took walks, he would always point out "pretty" rocks to me. He would pick them up and put them in my hand and say, "You better keep this one for your collection."

I had a collection of small pretty rocks in my bedroom and big ones in the yard.

Everyplace we went, I hunted for good rocks to add to my collection.

When we went fishing, I hunted for rocks.

When we went camping, I hunted for rocks.

When we went to visit friends, I hunted for rocks.

My daddy had turned me into a rock hound—that's someone who really likes rocks.

One day we took a drive in the country with my aunt and uncle and four little cousins. We went down a winding dirt road. We passed through miles of woods. Soon we came around a big curve and into an open field. In the field stood the biggest rock I had ever seen. It was as big as a house. There were tunnels in it and small holes just big enough for us to curl up and hide in. We looked like little birds in a nest. We played on the rock all afternoon and had a picnic there before going home.

We named our rock the Big Rock Candy Mountain after the song. We sang that song all the way home.

I was finding out that rocks are everywhere!

People built whole houses out of them. And they built fireplaces out of them.

Sometimes when we were driving around, my mama would spot a stone house. She would always tell my daddy that she would love to live in a stone house.

I thought they looked like a cottage in a fairy tale.

When we went camping, we always gathered rocks to put around our campfire. They kept the fire from spreading because rocks don't burn.

We liked to find flat rocks and skip them in the lake. We counted each skip to see who had the most skips. Sometimes we just threw rocks into the lake to see who could throw the farthest.

When I was about ten years old, someone had the idea to put small rocks in a box and sell them. They called them Pet Rocks.

One of my favorite things to do with rocks is use them in the garden. I put them around my flowers and made a path with them. I have a favorite one to sit on when I want to read.

Jewelry is made from rocks. Diamonds, rubies, and emeralds are all just rocks. Imagine that! When my daddy married my mama, he gave her a rock!

There are great big buildings made out of rock. If you look around, you can find rocks everywhere.

There are many wonderful rocks in the world, but my favorites are still the rocks my daddy put in my hand for my collection.

e|LIVE

listen|imagine|view|experience

AUDIO BOOK DOWNLOAD INCLUDED WITH THIS BOOK!

In your hands you hold a complete digital entertainment package. In addition to the paper version, you receive a free download of the audio version of this book. Simply use the code listed below when visiting our website. Once downloaded to your computer, you can listen to the book through your computer's speakers, burn it to an audio CD or save the file to your portable music device (such as Apple's popular iPod) and listen on the go!

How to get your free audio book digital download:

1. Visit www.tatepublishing.com and click on the elLIVE logo on the home page.
2. Enter the following coupon code:
    96a8-b6d3-cae8-b7a8-5018-8eeb-c0d1-ecd7
3. Download the audio book from your elLIVE digital locker and begin enjoying your new digital entertainment package today!